C0-DVG-200

I Will Search at Odd Angles

Just as the root of a plant might search deeply
or at odd angles
into the ground
for water.
so will I search deeply and against whatever
obstacles to find the source of my life: God.

102388

James Goedken

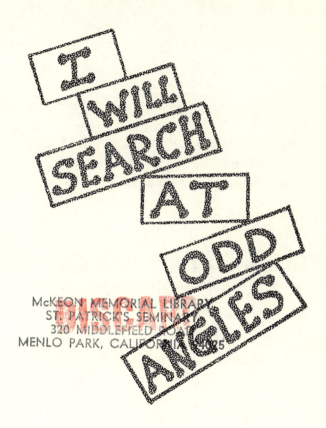

I WILL SEARCH AT ODD ANGLES

McKEON MEMORIAL LIBRARY
ST. PATRICK'S SEMINARY
320 MIDDLEFIELD ROAD
MENLO PARK, CALIFORNIA 94025

ALBA ◢BOOKS

BV
4850
·G63

Excerpts from the NEW AMERICAN BIBLE
© Confraternity of Christian Doctrine 1970
are used by permission of the copyright owner.

Library of Congress Catalog Card Number: 77-71023
ISBN   0 — 8189 — 1144 — 1

© Copyright, 1977 by Alba House Communications,
Canfield, Ohio, 44406

Printed in the United States of America

Artwork by Sister Ingrid Hottinger
Cover photo courtesy of Alba House Communications

The
Author

Fr. James Goedken took his Masters Degree in Literature at Mount St. Bernard College, Dubuque, Iowa and his M.R.E. at Seattle University before ordination to the priesthood in 1966.

He was Associate Pastor for five years and was then appointed to LaSalle High School, Cedar Rapids. He has been extremely active in recent years in Retreat and Marriage Encounter work, with Pre-Cana groups and as Director of Religious Education and CCD Workshops.

CONTENTS

FOREWORD

This book was written day by day over about two years. I am a priest. I am a High School Religion teacher. I pray for our students and with our students. At LaSalle High School in Cedar Rapids, Iowa, we begin each day with prayer, usually led by me, which comes on over the public address system.

Prayer must come directly from the heart. It has to bubble up from the soul of the person who really wants to have a vibrant relationship with God. Prayer must also come directly from life as the person praying sees it, feels it, enjoys it, is hurt by it, gives to it and receives from it.

So, I offer my prayers first of all to my God whom I love. Secondly, I offer them to others as one example of how a struggling Christian might speak to his God. Some prayers may sound dumb, others irrelevant. That's because they are MY prayers, not yours. You must try to pray your own way. I encourage you to do that, and more.

I wish to thank the students and staff members of LaSalle High School who inspired me to pray. I also thank Mr. Joel Gorun, who suggested that I publish this collection, and numerous friends like Joe and Cathy Connell who assisted me in one way or another. Above all I sincerely thank Sister Ingrid Hottinger who so generously gave her time and talents to make this book a reality.

James Goedken

December 8, 1976

asking

Lord God, Father of us all,
we beg for your attention
on this first day of the
school year.

Help us, Lord, to make this a good year.
Let it be a year that we'll be proud of at the end.

We want so much, Lord,
to be happy.
Guide us toward this goal.
Let learning be a joy
and a pleasure for us.
And remind us during those times
when it gets dull or frustrating
or painful
that we can still grow and learn
in spite of those factors.

We thank you, Lord, for bringing us here together.
Thank you for all our new students,
our new teachers, our new parking lot.
Thank you, Lord, for another year, another chance
to hear you and see you as we work
and play together.
Thank you, Lord, for this most amazing day.

**I will pour out my spirit upon mankind ... and I will
work wonders in the heavens and on the earth. Jl. 3:1-3**

Dear Lord, I want to talk to you about

HONESTY.

Please hear me when I pray that I be an honest person; it's so important, Lord, I'm really nobody without it.

But the temptation is so persistent to hide myself, to keep from really saying who I am.
I can lie in the most subtle ways,
so subtle that I'm surprised myself
afterwards when I recognize it.

Help me, Lord, to be

HONEST.

Love justice, you who judge the earth; think of the Lord in goodness, and seek Him in integrity of heart.
Wis. 1:1

4

Heavenly Father,
we want to pray.

We remind ourselves, Father, of all
you have done for us.

> *You have given us life,*
> > *love,*
> > > *laughter.*

> *You give us tall,*
> > *sinewy,*
> > > *agile people*
> *who can play good basketball.*
> *You give us happy,*
> > *enthusiastic*
> > > *kids*
> *who back them up.*

> *You give us happy,*
> > *healthy*
> > > *teachers*
> *who encourage all of them to do their very best.*

Father, we are going to rely
on your goodness to us in the past.

We thank you for it, of course, but now we're
asking more of the same.

And Father,
since we are presuming upon your generosity,
we pledge ourselves to be more generous too.

> > *Thank*
> > > *you,*
> > > > *Father.*

He who fears the Lord is never alarmed, never afraid,
for the Lord is his hope. **Sir. 34:14**

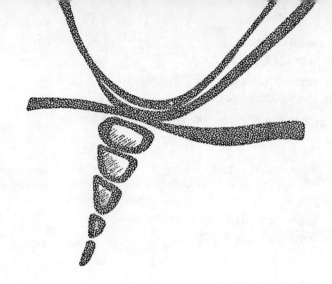

Lord God, pick me up and carry me across the
   cesspool of my weakness.

   Give me the strength to run through life
   without giving in to the pettiness
   I see around me.

   Make me a man of solid and stainless steel
   so that I will not succumb to the
   temptations of this world.

But . . . failing all this, as I am,
   I ask only that you teach me
   how to accept
   your forgiveness of me.

**Let us wash off all that can soil either body or spirit,
to reach perfection of holiness in the fear of God.**
                                              II Cor. 7:1

Reflect on this idea from St. Paul.

"TELL THOSE WHO ARE RICH IN THE
THINGS OF THIS LIFE NOT TO BE
PROUD, AND TO PLACE THEIR HOPE,
NOT IN SUCH AN UNCERTAIN THING
AS RICHES, BUT IN GOD WHO
GENEROUSLY GIVES US EVERYTHING
FOR US TO ENJOY. TELL THEM TO DO
GOOD, TO BE RICH IN GOOD WORKS,
TO BE GENEROUS AND READY TO
SHARE WITH OTHERS."

Let us pray...

Lord God, I want to be a generous person.
   I want to give.
   I think maybe I'm more concerned
   about what I'm going to get than
   I am about what I'm going to give.
   I don't like this in me.
   Please inspire me to change this.
   Transform me, Lord, from a
   "getting" person to a
   "giving" person.
   I praise you, Lord, and I thank you
   for the example of the giving people
   around me.
   Help me to be this way, too.

Why does fire fascinate me?

What is there in a flame that picks me up and carries me away to a new and different world?

Fire, in a fire place, on a candle, in a forest transforms me from a waiting person into a transcending person.

Fire, burns away the waste of me. It destroys hatred and ignorance. It purifies me from my laziness and cowardice.

Fire, consumes the old phoenix-bird of sin and selfishness; it gives birth to the new phoenix-bird of loving and creating.

When I was a child, I saw fire consume a farmer's barn. It burnt up old hay and straw. It killed four young calves. It wiped out everything that was there. But after it was all over, the farmer bull-dozed away the ashes and he built a new barn, bigger and more efficient than the old one. Something there is about fire that hurts and kills and cleanses and purifies and builds and makes new.

I speak to fire, as if it were a person, a god-person even; and I say:

> *"Change me, transform me, redeem me. Burn away my putrid hatefullness and give light and warmth to my love. Do this in me, fire, do this in me now."*

The voice of the Lord strikes fiery flames. . . .   **Ps. 29:7**

I pray to you, Lord. I ask you to help all struggling, searching people. Please help the person who wants very much to do what is right, but who sometimes does wrong.

Please help people who suffer disappointments and heartbreaks.

And Lord, thank you so very much for good things, like for example:

> *the senior girls who just finished making TEC. May they continue to meet your son Jesus in their lives.*

Finally, Lord, relying on your past kindness to us, and being thankful for such kindness, may we all move toward greater love and greater fulfillment in our lives.

I am sure of this much: that he who has begun the good work in you will carry it through to completion.
Phil. 1:6

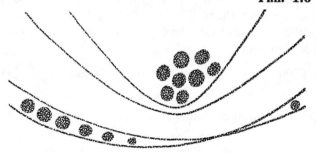

*Well, Lord, here we are, another
Monday morning, and we all figure
that we have much to do and many
things to think about.*

*Help us, Lord, to do what we can
to make this week a week we'll all
be happy about after it's over
with. Help us, Lord, to make it
a week of real growth—spiritual
and emotional growth—for the
whole school and everyone
involved.*

*We want to win, Lord, but even
more important, in the long run
anyway, is how we grow as
human beings and as Christian
people.*

*Lord, we beg of you, help us all:
team and school, to grow.
And we thank you, Lord, graciously,
for this opportunity.*

**Blest are they who hunger and thirst for holiness, they
shall have their fill.** Mt. 5:6

Lord, God, I am looking ahead.
I am looking around.

I think there must be a lot more
to life than what I see around me.

Keeping a good reputation,
studying hard,
getting ahead,
making money,

(oh yes, especially
making money)

seems to be just about all that I hear.

There has got to be more.

Tell me, Lord, once again the story
of love.

Tell me how a man gave up all that
He had, how He accepted a terrible
and humiliating death,
just so He could be true to Himself.

Tell me how He did this in order
to love.

Lord God, keep on reminding me of the beauty of
your goodness.

Jesus the Nazorean was a man whom God sent to you
with miracles, wonders, and signs. . . . **Acts 2:22**

Lord, is there anyone anywhere who knows
so much about being
alone
&
abandoned

that he cannot learn something about happiness
from people who are sick; or about fear from
people deeply in love; or about dreaming from
soldiers; or about courage from young people.

What I guess I'm asking, Lord, is for you to teach me.

Teach me
how to listen to the song of joy that
people in pain can sing.

Teach me
how to observe the trembling of fear in
people who seem to be on top of the world.

Teach me
how to see the visions that dying people see.

Teach me
how to be brave, brave like the unknowing
people are.

All who heard Him were amazed at His intelligence
and His answers. **Lk. 2:47**

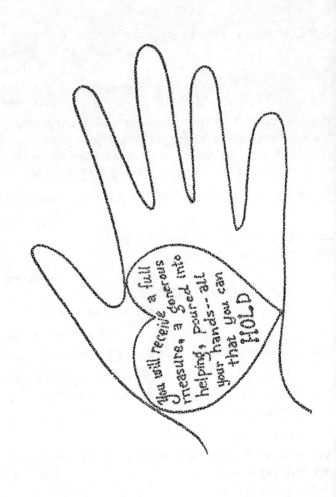

You will receive a full measure, a generous amount, poured into your hands—all that you can HOLD

Let's think about these words from Jesus:

"Do not judge others, and God will not judge you; do not condemn others and God will not condemn you; forgive others and God will forgive you. Give to others, and God will give to you: you will receive a full measure, a generous helping, poured into your hands—all that you can hold. The measure you use for others is the same measure God will use for you."

Luke 6:37-38

Lord God, help me to be a fair-minded person, giving to every man his due or maybe even more than his due.

Lord God, teach me to be more concerned about how I treat other folk than I am about how they treat me.

Finally, Lord, thank you for being so generous to me. It helps me to realize how much more generous I could be to others.

Dear Lord, I look to you for strength.

> *I do this because I know
> there are times when I am
> not adequate to the task
> of managing my life.*

*There are events that occur that I just
can't face alone.*

*There are sadnesses that I just can't
handle.*

*There are happinesses too big for my
heart.*

> *I guess what I'm saying, Lord,
> is that I need you.*
>
> *I hereby acknowledge that fact*
>
> *and*
>
> *I also declare my intention
> to put my trust in you.*

*I ask you to help me; and I thank you for
having helped me.*

**O Lord, you are our Father; we are the clay and you
the potter; we are all the work of your hands.   Is. 64:7**

Lord, I am tired.

And I imagine a lot of other people are, too.

> *But, I feel happy, and I feel grateful.*

> *I'm grateful, Lord, for a good
> Day of Renewal yesterday.*

*As a matter of fact, Lord, I want to take this
opportunity to thank you for all five of the
days that we've had.*

*It's impossible, Lord, as you know to assess
what they've really been worth ... but ...*

*they've been a lot more good than bad,
and that's something.*

> *So, thank you.*

*And now, presuming, Lord, on your past goodness
to us, I ask, I dare to ask, even more.*

*Please, Lord, I ask that all of us can take
something good out of all that's happened
and put it into our lives, and there let it live,
and grow, and praise you for ever and ever.*

**We pray for you always that God may make you worthy
of His call.**   **II Thess. 1:11**

Lord, you have asked me to be a man of prayer and
a man of love.

And I tell you, Lord Jesus, that it is my sincere
intention to fulfill your every wish.

Lord, I am praying now.

I am praying to you for the courage
I need in order to love.

I ask like Abraham Lincoln did, that I show
malice toward no one, and that I show
charity toward every one.

I am aware, Lord Jesus, that in order to be a man
of love, I definitely must also be a man of strength,
a man of self-discipline, and a man of great faith.
I cannot be a weakling. I cannot be wishy-washy.
I cannot be soft on myself. All of this calls
for super-human effort. And I guess that
that's what I'm asking for.

Please help me to do this.

From the cup I drink of, you shall drink.   Mt. 20:23

*Lord God, I pray to you because
I want to tell you about all those things
that are happening to me.*

*I want to tell you about the pain, the sadness
I feel when I see my mom and dad suffering.*

*I want to tell you about the love I feel
when I see them loving each other.*

*I want to tell you about the self-confidence
I feel when I know that I've helped someone
to feel better about themselves.*

*I want to tell you about the doubts I have,
and the lack of confidence I experience when
I get ridiculed and put down.*

*I want to tell you about the bitter-sweet
exhaustion I feel when I sure worked hard.*

*Lord God, I pray to you because I want
to tell you who I am.*

And, hey, thanks for listening; it's been great.

When I call out to the Lord, He answers me.　　**Ps. 3:5**

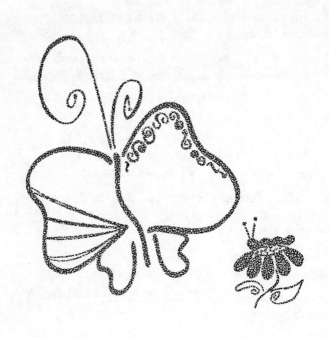

Let us pray.

Lord God, help me to understand life.

*I know there is much more to it than
basketball games and superbowl games.*

*Help me to understand birth and death,
rebirth and new life.*

Help me to see my own birth and my own life.

*And Lord, above all, help me to be ready for
my own death—
which I know is another
birth—*

a birth into a new life.

Whoever would preserve his life will lose it ... Mk. 8:35

Lord, help us walk through the mud and mire of
    confusion. Bring us into the light of
    happiness and fun.

Teach us, literally, how to make school a joy
    instead of a burden.

Inspire us teachers to give our very best
    in knowledge, humor, love and creativity.

Inspire us students to give our very best
    in these same things—they are
    so important for good classes.

Show us how to respect and revere each other
for the very special gifts that each of us has.

We love you, Lord, and we want to be our best
selves. Teach us how to achieve this. Please.

"If you are willing to listen, you will learn."   **Sir. 6:33**

Lord, help us find the right time.

We need time to celebrate;
sometimes to celebrate quietly and solemnly
and with dignity;
sometimes with loud happy music and
spirit-filled singing;
and sometimes even with profound sorrow
and soul-cracking sadness.

We need time to celebrate the right things:
things like love, joy, loss;
things like birth and death;
even things like growing up
and moving on to new places
and new attitudes.

Lord, help us to celebrate today with self-control
and discipline—the time to celebrate release and
relief is not yet here. It is coming, but not yet.

Help us find the right time for that.

"There is an appointed time for everything and a time for every affair under the heavens."   **Eccl. 3:1**

Well, Lord, here I am again.

> *I'm here with my hands out
> and my mouth open.*

*I have to admit, Lord, that I'm just about always
in the posture of a person receiving.*

I need, Lord.

I'm begging. I'm asking. I'm expecting. I'm waiting.

I am emptiness, waiting to be filled by you.

> *There are so many people, Lord,
> who are in situations much worse.*

> *What must they be doing?*

*Help me, Lord, to be conscious and aware of all those
other people who need your attention.*

Help me, Lord.

**O Lord, all my desire is before you; from you my
groaning is not hid.** **Ps. 38:10**

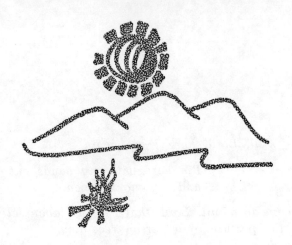

Well, Lord, we are getting very close to the end of the school year—tests all day today—no doubt.

We pray, Lord, that you help us bring to a good conclusion all the work that has been done this year.

Remind us, please, of the good things we have done.

Let us know that these tests only serve the purpose of reminding us of that—not condemning us.

Guide us through the summer and on into good and happy lives.

Oh, yes, thank you for all you have done for us over the past school year.

Yes, thank you, Lord, very much.

"For every way, O Lord! you magnified and glorified your people, unfailing, you stood by them in every time and circumstance." Wis. 19:22

*Ah, Lord, the last day of school
is here. We welcome it.*

*We need time to recreate, i.e., we need time to
re-create:*

> *to re-create ourselves,
> to re-create the direction of our lives,
> to re-create all that we stand for.*

*So, help us, Lord, to make the most of the
next three months.*

*Let it be a time of relaxation and fun,
a time to see people we've been
neglecting,
a time to wonder at the beauty of nature,
a time to share with people who need
our love,
a time to praise you, and thank you for
the fantastic mystery of life.*

Help us, Lord, to make the most of our precious time.

**"God looked at everything He had made, and He found
it very good."**   **Gen. 1:31**

searching

Lord, let me soar like an eagle, up above the
hills and the trees, up above the clouds, even.
    Let me see the place I live in from
far, far away.
    Let me be objective about all this.

Lord, let me crawl around in the soil
like an earthworm.
    Let me see what it's like
from close up.
    Let me get down-to-earth
about life.

And then, Lord, let me know the secrets of life.
                Let me know the secrets of love.
                Let all things be important to me.

Just as you know not how the breath of life fashions
the human frame in the mother's womb, so you know
not the work of God which He is accomplishing in
the universe.   **Eccl. 11:5**

Lord Jesus, I want to tell you this morning
of a search that is going on in my life.

I am looking,
I want to know,
I want to know what life is all about.

Sometimes, Jesus, it seems like a farce,
a riddle,
maybe even a bad joke.

At other times, it seems so very good, like a big
turn-on, like something beautiful and
a lot of fun.

Tell me, Lord Jesus, what is it, really?

Is it whatever I feel like at the moment?
But that doesn't make sense.

Is life something that I'm only beginning to
understand?

Is all my questioning and my switching back
and forth from good to bad a sign that
I don't know much about it at all?

I think so.

So I pray, Jesus, inspire me to continue looking,

searching,
asking,
enjoying,
and
experiencing.

**Come, let us climb the mount of the Lord, to the house
of Jacob, that He may instruct us in His ways. Mic. 4:2**

My Lord, this morning
  I thought about the beginning of life—

how through eons of time
life slowly began to be,

and then after a much longer time,
  a time perhaps so long that it would be
  difficult for the human mind to calculate,
but after this time
consciousness began to develop.

Would it have been Adam who first thought
thoughts like:

  "Who am I?"

  "What am I doing here?"

  "What is life all about anyway?"

  Well, Lord, if it were him,
you can tell him from me that we are still asking
the same questions!

  And then, Lord, when I had said that,
  it occurred to me:

  "Why, of course, we're only a few
  evolutionary minutes away
  from him anyway."

  Ah, Lord, it is true:
your thoughts are not my thoughts—my thoughts
not yours.

How silly, how vain of me to think
they might have been.

**The Lord God formed man out of the clay of the
ground and blew into his nostrils the breath of life.**
Gen. 2:7

Lord, I am probing into the mysteries of life.
I ask you to be with me as I search.

I want to know why the mind works
so well sometimes and then at other times fails
so miserably. I mean there are times when
I surprise myself with what I know, and then
there are other times when I can barely
remember my name.

I want to know how the heart can be so loving,
so generous, so beautiful on certain occasions;
and then at other times so selfish and mean,
so petty and vengeful.

Hey, why is that? Why is that???

Lord, give me some answers, please?!?

"May He who is the Lord of peace give you continued peace in every possible way." II Thess. 3:16

Lord, we pray for your guidance. I think
that the world is all a bit crazy.

People seem to want the strangest things.

They work terribly hard to get money, and more
money.
But then when they do get all that money,
they still aren't happy.

Help us, Lord, to discover in our own stupid ways
just what it is that makes us happy.

Help us to know, help us to follow that quest
no matter how difficult it is to follow—
no matter where it takes us.

Never let us give up the search.

And thank you, Lord, for the ability and the
freedom to search.

Thank you, Lord.

How blest are the poor in spirit: the reign of God is theirs. **Mt. 5:3**

Lord God, you know who I am.

What shall I do?

*Lately, Lord, I've been too busy
to really talk to you—and I'm
sorry about that.*

*I've also been
troubled inside myself—too
troubled to talk to you.*

*There is this problem—about
which, it seems, I can't talk
to anyone—except you.*

*I am grateful, Lord, that you
do hear me, and love me—even
when I don't talk to you.*

*I wish I could tell you more,
but, anyway, please hear me,
                love me,
                wait for me.*

**I would speak with the almighty; I wish to reason with
God.** **Job 13:3**

Lord, it seems like I am unable to pray.

I have tried to speak to you but I can't find any words.

I know I need your love, now, more than at any other time.

I feel separated, estranged and very much alone.

Help me, Lord, to deal with this.
Perhaps you are telling me to grow up a little more, to be less dependent.

Whatever it is, Lord, I accept it.

"Lord, teach us how to pray."   **Lk. 11:1**

*Lord, I know that my life is beset with
choices that I must make every day.*

Some are easy—others more difficult.

*Please help me and support me when
I must make one of those really tough ones.*

*Give me the strength to say "Yes" when
I believe that it is best;
even though to say "No" would be
so much easier.*

Please, Lord, give me this strength.

*And then, Lord, if I can presume
to ask more,
give me the perseverance to follow
through on choices I have made.*

**"My Father, if it is possible, let this cup pass me by.
Still, let it be as you would have it, not as I." Lk. 22:42**

Lord, there is something inside of me that is
screaming to be released.

Sometimes it makes me feel confused,
and I don't know what to do with it.

Sometimes I get very excited because of it
and I sing or shout or jump up and down.

Other times this powerful, unnamed feeling
bubbles softly to the surface and I feel
like being quiet, like just sitting down
alone somewhere to enjoy it.

Could it be my real self, inside, trying
to respond to the sound of your voice,
gently reverberating in my heart?

**"My being proclaims the greatness of the Lord. My
spirit finds joy in God my Savior."** Lk. 1:46-47

Lord, I want to think about the good things—about
    fun and excitement.

    I want to think about adventure and courage
    —how about life as it could be lived
    on top of a mountain?

Well, now that is a tough thought.

    Living on top of a mountain sure sounds
    beautiful, exciting, and all the rest.

But it also sounds meager and very difficult.

I ask myself, I say, "Self, do you really want to be
    that self-disciplined? It won't be easy
    you know."

Well, Lord, in the end it's all a question of
what you want—and what you are
willing to give isn't it?

Help me, Lord, please, to reach high—
    and then be willing to pay high, too.

    Right?

Good things, really good things, just do not
come easy.

'The kingdom of heaven is like a merchant's search for
fine pearls. When he found one really valuable pearl,
he went back and put up for sale all that he had and
bought it."   Mt. 13:45-46

Lord, I am aware of a lot of stupid mistakes
in my life.

   I feel them in my gut at the end of a school day.

   Embarrassment
         and
      shame burn hot on my face.

When I feel like this, Lord God, I want
to run away and hide.

                    So...

I need some help, some direction.
I need to think about all this so I can figure it out.

      When is a mistake just something I should
                                    laugh off?
      When is the mistake a sin?

Help me, Lord, to find the meaning of it all.

Finally, Lord, I do confess my guilt because I know
that I have done wrong.

                    Forgive me...

And make of me a new man.

Thank you, Lord, for your forgiving me. It makes
me feel sort of worthwhile again.

**A clean heart create for me, O God, and a steadfast
spirit renew within me.** **Ps. 51:12**

Lord God, I seek to know you better,
to love you more.

I find it difficult, however, to keep on trying
to stretch myself. The pains and frustrations of just
plain living weigh me down.

When I feel abandoned, or alienated, or unloved,
then I find it impossible to reach out to you.
And yet I know that that is exactly the time when,
for my own good, I must stretch myself
and reach out to you.

Help me, Lord, to stretch.

"Return to me, and I will return to you," says the
Lord of hosts. Mal. 3:7

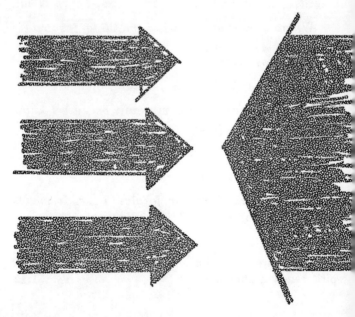

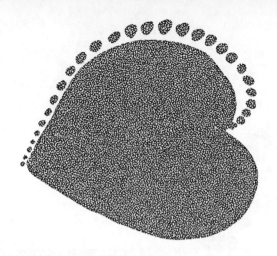

*Lord, I'm here looking for you
in my life.*

*I see you clearly some days
and then again ... well ...*

   I'm waiting.

*I know, Lord. Sometimes you
want me to grow—and I must grow.*

*So maybe all I can say today is:
please help me to be patient.*

Patient with you and patient with me.

*I hope I don't sound merely polite
when I say, "Thank you" for all
you've done and been for me in
the past because I want to
sincerely say, "Thank you."*

Love is patient; love is kind.   **I Cor. 13:4**

Lord, I need your help.
I guess I even need your assurance
that I'm all right.

Please help me to direct my life
in a good direction.

It seems so easy for me to go astray
and kind of forget about you.

Lord, my need for you is sometimes desperate.

I feel that way right now.

And, Lord, I know you hear.
All my past experiences tell me that.
I know that you are aware of me, and more,
that you love me very much.

For this I am very grateful.

He who lives in me and I in him, will produce abundantly. **Jn. 15:5**

Jesus spoke to me when he said:

"COME TO ME, ALL OF YOU WHO ARE TIRED
FROM CARRYING YOUR HEAVY LOADS,
AND I WILL GIVE YOU REST. TAKE MY NECK
YOKE AND PUT IT ON YOU, AND LEARN
FROM ME, BECAUSE I AM GENTLE AND
HUMBLE IN SPIRIT; AND YOU WILL FIND
REST. THE YOKE I WILL GIVE YOU IS EASY,
AND THE LOAD I WILL PUT ON YOU
IS LIGHT."

Let us pray . . .

Lord Jesus, I am a proud and selfish man.
I worry about all the wrong things.
I worry about how I look and how I sound
before others.

Help me to put aside these vain and conceited
ambitions.

Show me how to surrender myself to you.

Lord Jesus, you are in charge of me.

Let me find security and self-fulfillment only
in you.

Lord, I am conscious of your gaze.

*I've been thinking about how your "word"
is living and effective,*

"that it is sharper than any two-edged sword."

I know that nothing is concealed from you.

*Therefore I have no choice but to open
my entire life to you.*

*Sometimes I try to hide from you—
and right now I realize how totally
foolish that is.*

*Don't, please don't, ever let me make that
stupid mistake again.*

Lord, I tell you who I am so that

I may know who I am.

Thank you for your steady gaze.

Thank you for your total concern.

**"I am the Alpha and the Omega, the first and the last,
the beginning and the end."** Rev. 22:13

Lord, I'm thinking of some strange questions again.

Tell me, how can some people be upset about how little money they make when they are actually making more than 85% of the rest of the people of the world?

How can some people really be concerned about the amount of protein their pet dogs receive when 60% of the people in the world do not receive even the minimum needed to be healthy?

Why, Lord, why are there such gross inequities? And why are the greediest people apparently the most blessed in terms of material goods?

Are you trying to tell us something about the value of things—and how it has nothing really to do with the value of human life?

Is that it, Lord? If it is, why are we so darned slow to catch on?

We were left to feel like men condemned to death so that we might trust, not in ourselves, but in God who raises the dead.   **II Cor. 1:9**

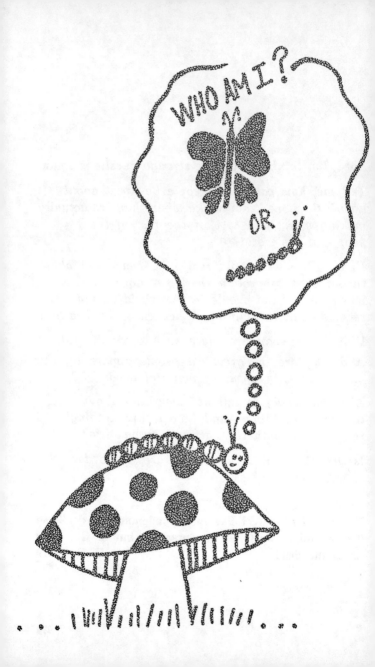

Please, Lord, teach me to know who I am.
I figure, by now, that I'll never meet the
President or the Pope! but I hope to meet
the real me.

I know I'll never be a big name
but can I be the real me, can I really
find the real me?

Lord, help me look to people younger than me;
like maybe to the high school kids I see
around me; maybe they can tell me who I
really am.

Lord, help me to look at my colleagues,
help me to ask the teachers I work with,
maybe they can tell me who I am.

And, really, Lord, if I listened more
to you, as you speak to me, I admit
I'd probably know more about who I am.

Help me, Lord, to have a sense of humor
about who I am.

**One cannot lessen, nor increase, nor penetrate the
wonders of the Lord.**   Sir. 18:4

hoping

Listen to these words from the famous Russian novelist, Tolstoy.

"Jesus Christ teaches men that there is something in them which lifts them above this life with its hurries, its pleasures and its fears. He who understands Christ's teachings feels like a bird that did not know it has wings and now suddenly realizes that it can fly, can be free, and no longer needs to fear."

Let us pray:

Lord Jesus, give to each of us this truth, the truth that will make us free: free from our fears, free from our ignorance, and free from all the limitations of hate and suspicion.

We know this truth is in your teaching. Help us, Jesus, to find it and make it a part of our lives.

Look! There is the lamb of God who takes away the sins of the world!   **Jn. 1:29**

In the gospel of John,
Jesus says to us:

> "REMEMBER, YOU DID NOT CHOOSE ME.
> I CHOSE YOU.
> AND I INTEND FOR YOU TO GO OUT
> AND BEAR FRUIT,
> THE KIND OF FRUIT THAT
> WILL ENDURE."

Lord God, I feel fear.
I don't think that I'm able to do this.
I'm afraid I cannot "bear fruit" even though
Jesus asks me to.

But Lord,
I also feel a kind of confidence
in knowing that your Son Jesus chooses me.
I must be wrong about thinking that I am not able
because He apparently thinks I am
or He would not have chosen me.
And, gee, He ought to know!

Father,
I feel comfort in relying upon Jesus' choice of me.
Thank you, Lord, Thank you, Jesus
because you chose me.
I hope I am worthy of the confidence
you have placed in me.

Well, Lord, I feel O.K.

*I don't always feel good
but right now I do.*

*I think I do because of the hope
that I see,*

> *because of the hope
that is inside of me,*
>
> *because of the hope
that you seem to pull out of me.*

*I feel grateful, Lord, because your generosity has
gently reached into my heart,*

> *touching,
soothing,
warming me.*

*I feel loved, Lord, because you and some
of your good people have told me so.*

*Thank you, Lord, and let me respond to you
by sharing this goodness with
all of your people everywhere.*

**Beside restful waters He leads me; He refreshes my
soul.   Ps. 23:2**

*God, You are the source of all light
and goodness.*

*Help me to see things as they really are,
not just as others tell me, and not
just as I want them to be.*

*O God, I know how I can kid myself
and make myself believe what
I want to.*

*So help me, please, to see
what is really there.*

Teach me to be humble before the truth.

Teach me to be open before the truth.

Keep on assuring me of this simple fact:

no truth can ever lead me away from you.

Truth can only lead me toward you.

*God, please give me the confidence
to believe that with all my heart.*

*And then give me, please, that extra
confidence to act on it.*

I am the Way, the Truth, and the Life.   **Jn. 14:6**

teach us to pray

Lord, I find it hard to pray.

*My body aches, my spirit is numb,
my mind is a vacuum.*

*I would like to say thank you,
but I cannot.*

*I want to praise you,
but the thoughts and the words
do not come out of me.*

*For today, Lord, I can only say,
as others have,*

"Lord, teach us how to pray."

*H-m-m-m. Isn't that peculiar?
I didn't think I could pray
but
by God, I did!*

A patient man need stand firm but for a time, and then contentment comes back to him.   **Sir. L:20**

Dear Lord, I'm thinking again
about the life you give us.
It is fragile and beautiful.
But then most fragile things
are very beautiful, aren't they?

But it seems like I treat life,
and I mean my very own life,
as if it were made of steel
blocks rather than of fine crystal.

Life is precious; as precious
as the smile on the tear-stained
face of a child.

Life is delicate; as delicate
as the fiber of a cob web.

I know this, Lord, I know it
as surely as I know the sun rises;
but dumb me,
I forget it now and then.

I've been ignoring these facts
for a long time now—
but not anymore.

Lord, now I remember and I
will never forget.
I praise you, Lord, and I thank you

for making life so fragile,
                    so precious,
                    so delicate.

. . . You are the God of the lowly . . . the Savior of those without hope.   **Jdt. 9:11**

Lord, help us to be patient,
to wait,
to really wait

for your fullness and love

to completely fill us.

We long for you,
we are anxious for you
to show yourself to us,

but,

I guess, as is the case with
all good things,
we must wait.

I just want you to know, Lord,
that it isn't always easy...

Sometimes I even think ungratefully, that it's
pretty inconsiderate of you to keep us all waiting.

But then, Lord, I remind myself
that there is so much to learn before
we can even begin to know who you really are...

let alone face up to you directly.

Help us, Lord, to be patient, to be patient,
to be patient.

God is wise in heart and mighty in strength; who has withstood Him and remained unscathed? **Job 9:4**

Lord, I can't pray.

I want to.

I want to talk to you and tell you who I am.
I want to tell you about how I hope for better
        things in this life.

I hope for more smiles.
I hope for more statements like:

"Let me tell you what I think."

                and

"Hey, I'm interested in what you know about this."

I hope for, O my God, I hope for Spring,
for shirt-sleeve weather,
for hikes in the country,
canoeing, and
camp-outs.

I hope for a new life where I can jump and
run and laugh and swim and lie in the sun,
soaking up warmth.

Say, Lord, you haven't answered any of these
"hopes" I have—except for the first one.
I asked to be able to pray—and you let me do it.

Thanks. I needed that.

I love the Lord because He has heard my voice.
                                        Ps. 116:1

65

Lord God, I want to tell you who I am, because, it seems to me that that is a good way to tell someone you love them.

So, Lord, hear me. I am one of your humans down here on that little planet, the one we call earth. (I wonder what you call it??! Oh, well...)

I am very much like all the rest of the humans here. I try hard but I fail maybe half the time. I am loved by others but I usually think I'm not, and so I suffer quite a bit from that.

I have about everything I could ever need but I still seem to want more.

I tell other humans to trust me, but I often find it difficult to trust them.

I tell other people how good it is when we are all honest and truthful to one another; and then I'm the first to fail them.

I suppose I was created to succeed miserably, and to fail gloriously, but I still hold out for something better.

Well, that's it for now, Lord. Maybe I'll really get around to something better another day. OK?? I trust you'll wait for me, since you are better at that than I am.

O God, you know my folly, and my faults are not hid from you.   **Ps. 69:6**

The gospel is a message of hope.
The gospel invites us to love and serve God.
The gospel invites us into a personal
*   relationship with Jesus Christ.*
The gospel is realistic in recognizing evil
*   and personal sin, yet it affirms hope*
*   that things can be better.*

Let us pray.

Lord, we all want things to be better,
at least, we're always saying that we do.

We sometimes try to make them better,
we sometimes sit back and do nothing,
we sometimes get caught up in our little
*   problems (or our big problems)*
*   and figure that there's nothing we can do.*

But Lord, there is something we can do.
There are many things:

> *we can be truthful,*
>
> *we can be gentle,*
>
> *we can work hard,*
>
> *we can care about people.*

Lord, help us. Give us the strength to do just
*   these four simple things.*

God is rich in mercy; because of his great love for us he brought us to life with Christ when we were dead in sin.   **Eph. 2:4-5**

Lord, I want to thank you
for being present in my life.

I know you are present—
you waved at me and called
out to me yesterday afternoon
as I left school.

I know you are present—
last night you talked to me
from your heart, you told
me about some things that
are important to you; you
accepted me and you listened
to me when I told you about
some things that are very
important to me.

Thank you, Lord, for being
present in my life.

"God indeed is my Savior; I am confident and unafraid."
Is. 12:2

68

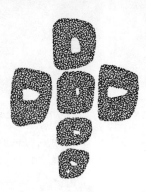

From out of the depths I cried to you, O Lord.

Lord, I said, hear my voice.

Let your ears attend to the sound of my supplication.

If you, O Lord, remember our sins, Lord,
    who can survive it?

But in your hands is the forgiveness of sins.

I trust in the Lord; my soul trusts in His word.

Let us pray:

Lord, I'm grateful to you because you heard.

I was sick, desperately sick in my soul.

But you heard me, you came and touched me
    and now I'm healed.

Thank you, Lord.

I'll remember this always.

Inspired by Psalm 130

Let's take time out to consider who we are:

Lord God, I realize that you created me and
after you did it you must have said,
"It is good."

Anyway you always said this after anything
or anybody you created.

You said this after you created man—
And I am a man, I am a person.

And I thank you, Lord, for creating me,
even though, everytime you turn me loose
I seem to do the same thing as the first man—
I create the original sin.

Well, Lord, if I didn't know this I'd probably quit.
But since I do know this—well, heck—there's
probably no stopping me in what I can do:
with your help.

Thank you, Lord, for your help.

And, please, continue to be there, O.K.?

**All of you who have been baptized into Christ have
clothed yourselves with Him.**   **Gal. 3:27**

*Well, Lord, thank you
for another vacation.*

I enjoyed it.

*The celebration of the Easter mysteries
was good for me.*

*As a matter of fact, I could've taken more of it—
and more time off from school, too, for that matter.*

*But I am happy about
it all.*

*Help all of us now, Lord, to really make
the best of the next two months.
Help us to see your activity in the arrival of spring
just around the corner...I hope!
Help us to look for and to find a real pleasure
in learning because that's what we've
come here for.*

*Thanks again, Lord for being
so good to us.*

**He has been raised from the dead and now goes ahead
of you....** Mt. 28:7

believing

Lord, I believe.

> *I believe in you and*
> *what you have done in me.*

> *I believe in peace.*
> *I work for peace even when it*
> *seems impossible to attain.*

> *I believe in being generous.*
> *I want to be a giving person,*
> *not a taking person.*

> *I believe in loving,*
> *without this there isn't*
> *anything on earth that*
> *makes any sense.*

> *I believe in your people,*
> *even the ones that upset me,*
> *and lie to me.*

Lord, I believe in you and I believe in me.

Please Lord, help me to deal with unbelief.

I am not ashamed of the Gospel, it is the power of God leading everyone who believes in it to salvation.
Rom. 1:16

All of the world looks to God for life,
                              for meaning,
                              for beauty.

Just as the root of a plant might search deeply,
                              or at odd angles
                              into the ground
                              for water,
so will I search deeply and against whatever
obstacles to find the source of my life: God.

Just as a tree will bend and contort itself to find
the sunlight, so will I go out of my way,
turn myself in-side-out actually, to find the light
in the darkness of my life: Jesus Christ,
                              the light
                              of all life.

> *O God, I praise you*
> *and sing out alleluia*
> *to your name—*
> *because you are*
> *the source of life—*
> *particularly mine.*

**I believe that I shall see the bounty of the Lord in the
land of the living.**   **Ps. 27:13**

Lord God, my Father, I believe in you.

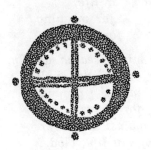

> I believe in your creativity
> and in your redemption.

> I believe your son, Jesus,
> is my brother
> who comes to me with a
> message of love from you.

> I also believe that your
> Spirit is alive and
> active in this world.

This faith, Lord, is beautiful.

> It is freeing.

> It is powerful.

It is because of this faith in you, Father,
that I can believe in myself;
in my own creativity,
in my own redeeming and healing ability.

I can say even, my God, believe in the power
I have to love. It's fantastic, Lord.

I am grateful.

"Because I believed, I spoke." We believe and so we speak.   **II Cor. 4:13**

Today, Jesus,
I want to talk
to you about

faith.

I recall an incident from the gospel.
One time you asked this man if he believed you.

And, Lord, he said, "I believe, help my unbelief."

Well,
I think
I can
identify with that man.
I can because
I often
feel
the same
way.

What I'm saying, Lord, is that what you ask of me,
too, is sometimes pretty tough to give.

Do I believe?
Yes I do!

But ... I ask, help me to give this to you with more
confidence, with a more profound commitment.

You see, Lord, I have given myself over to you—
completely. But then everytime that life gets
a little rough I keep taking back for myself
what I have given to you.
Don't let me do that. O.K.?

I believe, Lord!
Help my unbelief.

Lord, I hear a sound, it comes from a long,
long way from here.

And yet the sound is clear, as clear as a bell
ringing on a mountain top. The sound is like
the voice of a child calling to a playmate
several blocks away. There are no distinguishable
words in the sound—but the plaintive emotions
of it are unmistakable. The sound attracts me,
it calls out to me and bids me to approach.

Deep down in the finest recesses of my being
there is a yearning to follow the call,
to seek the source of the sound.

Lord, I ask you, send me. Send me to the place
from where this sound issues. I think Lord,
it may be the sound of your voice.

Lord, I want to answer. Lord, I will answer!

I am here.

I am coming!

Speak, Lord, for your servant is listening.   **I Sm. 3:9**

I BELIEVE

Lord God, I believe in you.

> I believe that you love me
> and
> forgive me.

> I believe that your concern for me
> is so wonderfully profound that
> I'll never really understand it.

But that's O.K., because it allows me to be
enthralled with the mystery of your deep caring.

Sometimes, usually when I'm not
feeling so very good about myself,
I fear that you no longer care for me.

But then during times of serenity, like now,
I firmly believe that your care for me is so
profound, so far-reaching that it goes way
beyond most of the petty, dumb, superficial
things I worry about.

> It's at times like this that I really
> appreciate your concern for me.

**Whoever believes in me, though he should die, will come
to life.**   **Jn. 11:26**

Lord Jesus, we kid ourselves.

We very much need a Savior.

*I say we kid ourselves because we usually
pretend like we have no need of you.*

> *We build buildings,
> we fly huge airplanes,
> we send powerful rockets out into space*

> *and then we say,
> like the fool:*

> *"There is no God."*

*We think like this because we have done
such tremendous things.*

*But then, Lord, there are some things
that we have not done.*

*We still have the job to do;
we still need to put an end to suffering.
We still need to declare once and for all
an end to things like*

> *Jealousy,
> Hatred,
> Distrust,
> Infighting,
> Back-biting,
> and a whole lot of other such things.*

*Lord, we need to be saved.
And we are asking you to do that for us.*

The fool says in his heart, "There is no God."   Ps. 53:2

83

Well, Lord, I'm here again.

I want to speak to you today about people who laugh, and people who make me laugh.

Maybe we humans think we're the only beings around who have a sense of humor. I'll bet you're the funniest person possible. Since you are all-good, all-mighty and all-powerful, I'll bet you're also all-funny. You've gotta have a terrific sense of humor to do some of the things you've done.

Like, why do ducks waddle when they walk? Is it to offset the grace they possess when they swim?

Why do humans look so odd when they're embarrassed? Is it to offset the self-righteousness they have when they know they are, oh, so right?

We praise you, Lord God, for being so funny, and we really appreciate your sharing your humor with us. Thanks.

God looked at everything He had made, and He found it very good. **Gen. 1:31**

suffering

Lord, I want to tell you something.

*Nothing has been going very well for me
lately. It seems like everytime I begin
a conversation with anyone they only tell
me bad things. I'm listening to complainers
and whiners all the time.*

And Lord...

*When I look at myself and try to
remember what I've been talking
about lately I guess I'm forced to admit
that I do a lot of griping too.*

Lord,

Help me to see things in a better light.

*Even in the death of winter your world
is beautiful.
Even with what seems like a lot of
school work, teaching and learning
is good for me.*

*What I guess I'm saying, Lord, is
I want you to help me to rise above the
blahs of the season.*

*Help me to enjoy life
and praise you for its goodness.
Thank you, Lord.*

I believed, even when I said, "I am greatly afflicted."
Ps. 116:10

Lord, some days life is really a mess.

> *Everything goes wrong—and then*
> *when you think you're at the end*
> *of your rope*
> *something else happens.*

On days like that we can only save ourselves
by recalling your day—a day of death.

And isn't it ironic, Lord Jesus, that we
should take that terrible day,
> *that humiliating Friday*
when everything went wrong for you
and we should name that Friday Good.

> *If you can stand that final dishonor*
> *then I figure there must be something*
> *in it for us.*

There's a lesson here, Lord.

> *Help*
> *me*
> *to*
> *know*
> *it*
> *deep*
> *down*
> *in*
> *my*
> *heart.*

When they had crucified Him, they divided His clothes
among them by casting lots.   **Mt. 27:35**

Lord, I'm sorry that I tend
to forget about you.

I don't mean to,
but then it does
happen.

Well, right now I'm not forgetting
about you.

I feel deeply, Lord,
a thankfulness I am
not starving to death
at the moment,
(actually I'm over-fed).

I am not struggling
with a grief that is
over-whelming me:

like a mother, father,
son, daughter so
violently killed
through someone else's
cruelty or negligence.

I'm not wandering
around homeless,
wondering where I'm
going to sleep tonight.
I have a good bed.

Lord, I'm so well-off.
I feel selfish in just
being who I am.

The Lord lifts up all who are falling and raises up all who are bowed down.   **Ps. 145:14**

*Lord God, I'm still thinking about all the hard stuff
you seem to expect me to do.*

*And...well...what I wish you would do is...
well...lay off.
I mean get off my back!*

Life is tough enough.

*I never planned to be some kind of saint and
you know, too, that I'm not making that.*

*But you say I haven't even hardly begun even.
Well, whaddaya want?*

More??

You do seem persuasive.

O.K., O.K., I'll try.

That's not good enough?

*All right, God, I accept.
I accept what you ask of me.
Yes, I'll do my very best.
But you have to help me, O.K.?
You will?
Fine.*

I'll do it.

**"Though I know my complaint is bitter, His hand is
heavy upon me in my groanings."** Job 23:2

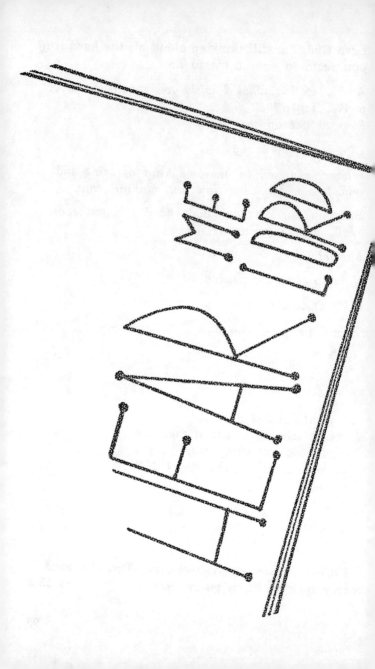

Hear me Lord.

I call out to you.

I'm calling to you with a voice of pain,
because I am filled with feelings of

Loneliness,

Betrayal,

Frustration,

and

Suffering of all kinds.

I speak to you, Lord, because it seems like
you are the only one left to hear me.

I am desperate. I am filled with needs.
I am emptied of all strength and self-worth.

I am not, any longer, who I am. I am not me.
I am every man—every son, every daughter
you have created.

We are lost, Lord, we need you.
We need you so much that we don't even
know how much.

Help us, Lord, help us.

My soul is deprived of peace, I have forgotten what
happiness is.   **Lam. 3:17**

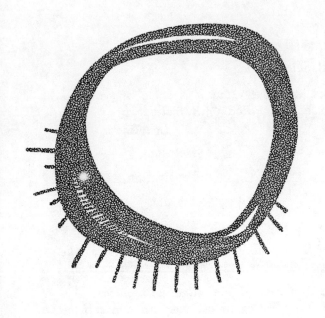

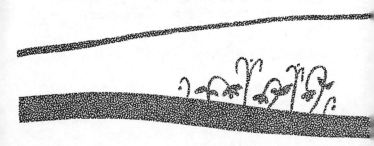

Lord, we come before you to pray.

The snow that covers everything everywhere seems to symbolize the oppression that we feel when we separate ourselves from you.

Take me back, Lord, into your good grace. Forgive me for straying away from you.

Help me now, Lord, to be always with you.

Give me back the joy of your salvation, and a willing spirit sustain in me. **Ps. 51:14**

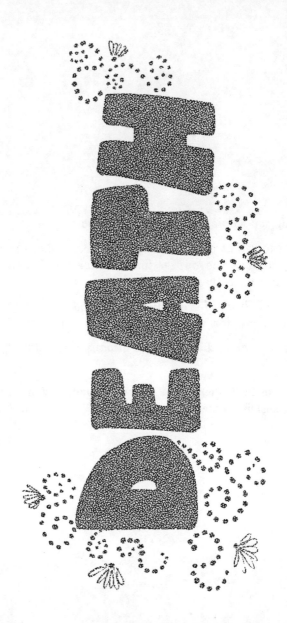

*I invite you to listen to this dark
message from Thomas More.*

"CONSIDER WELL THAT BOTH BY NIGHT
AND DAY WHILE WE MOST BUSILY
PROVIDE AND CARE FOR OUR DISPORT,
OUR REVEL, AND OUR PLAY FOR PLEASANT
MELODY AND DAINTY FARE, DEATH
STEALETH ON FULL SLILY: UNAWARE
HE LIES AT HAND AND SHALL US ALL
SURPRISE, WE KNOW NOT WHEN NOR
WHERE NOR IN WHAT WISE."

Let us pray...

> *Lord, I don't often think of death.
> Why, when it's my very own death,
> the end of my life as I know it now?
> I guess I almost never think of it.
> And frankly, I don't really want to
> think of it right now, except maybe
> to ask you to be there with me when
> it comes.*
>
> *I'd appreciate that. Thank you.*

... For you are dirt and to dirt you shall return.
Gen. 3:19

Listen to me, Lord. I need to be heard.

> *I need to be told that somehow*
> *things will be all right.*

You see, Lord, it looks like everything is
turning out wrong.

Why can't stuff happen the way I want it to
> *at least once in a while?*

Why can't life be more like it was last summer?
That was really neat.
I had some time to myself.
I could plan things then and have some kind of
assurance that they would take place sort of
the way I expected.
That was good, Lord.

> *But now ... now???*
> *Now I'm letting things get me down.*
> *I'm letting the teasing of friends*
>   *bother me.*

> *(Come to think of it—they teased me*
> *a lot last summer, too, only then I*
> *kind of enjoyed it. It made me feel good.)*
> *Why not now—why not?*

I guess I'm getting too wrapped up in myself.
Help me, Lord God, to unwind.
Help me to laugh at myself—let me have a
good long deep belly-laugh just because of who I am.
And then maybe things will go better, too.

> *Help me, Lord, to do this.*
> *And ... thanks for last summer.*
> *Thanks for today.*

Is not man's life on earth a drudgery? Are not his days
those of a hireling? **Job. 7:1**

Thank you, Lord, for the beautiful day yesterday.
I really enjoyed walking around in the warm air
without a coat on, without bracing myself
against a chilling wind, without
hurrying somewhere to get
inside.

Lord, there's one thing I want to ask you about:

Why are so many people often so unhappy?

Help them, Lord, help them to slow down
and enjoy life.
And help me to do this, too, Lord.

And help all those poor people over there
in foreign lands. They're really in some
terrible situations.

We people sure can be awful to each other, can't we?

Lord, we look always to you for help because
you are the Lord of heaven and earth and all that is.

We have the freedom and apparently the ability
to really mess things up—just help us, Lord,
Please help us to not be so cruel to each other.

Maybe it's our cruelty toward one another that
makes so many people so unhappy.
If we could only do something about that,
I think we'd all be a lot happier.

So, please, help us.

Return, O my soul, to your tranquility, for the Lord
has been good to you.   **Ps. 116:7**

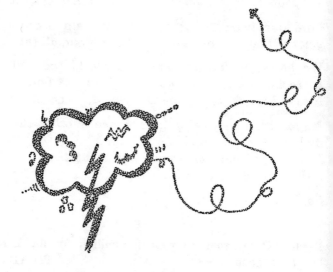

Lord, I am restless.
I've had my fill of piddly papers and broken chairs
and hallways full of debris.
I don't want any more noise
or icy stares
or hate-filled students.

Lord, I want to move out of this storm into the
calm of your presence.
    I want to feel the breeze on my face
and the sunshine on my bare back.
    I want to feel the cool clean spray
of mountain-stream water on my bald head.

Free me, Lord, from these walls and halls,
from all this frustration and confusion.

But, Lord, when I get there, if I could,
would I still know things like patience,
                                 discipline,
                                 forgiveness?

Maybe, what you want me to do is to stay right here
where I am, and tough it out. Right?

Well, I say with your Son, then:

"YOUR WILL BE DONE—NOT MINE," because
your will is better,   definitely better than mine.

Just help me accept it, O.K.?

Still, let it be as you would have it, not as I.   Mt. 26:39

Lord, I realize I have sinned.

I've done wrong and I admit it.

I beg for your forgiveness.

Sin has troubled me greatly. And when my own sin comes to my own attention, I am overcome with guilt and remorse.

Until you forgive me, Lord, I am deep in the pain of shame and guilt. How could I have ignored you and your people?

But you do forgive me.

As you say even if my sin is red as crimson you will make it white as wool.

Thank you, Lord, for forgiving me.

It's terrific to realize that I can still be all right even though I've been terrible in the past.

Thank you, Lord.

Though I am afflicted and poor, yet the Lord thinks of me. Ps. 40:18

Lord, I feel sad; not depressed, not frustrated,
just plain sad. I said good-bye to a friend
last night, to a friend that I'll probably
never see again. And I feel sad.

It's like a big part of the inside of me
got ripped out and sent to someplace else.
It hurt, Lord, it really hurt.

Maybe, Lord, you've felt the same way.

Like when your father died, like when your
good friend, Judas, betrayed you, like when
the temple bosses turned on you, or like
when all those people, no doubt you knew
some of them, laughed at you while you
hung on the cross dying.

Thank you, Lord Jesus, for helping me understand—
even if just a little bit—still, thank you
for helping me understand.

My comfort in my affliction is that your promise gives me life.   **Ps. 119:50**

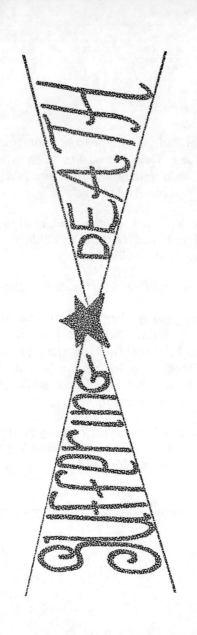

Lord, it's about this constitutional inability I have.

I hate to see people suffer.

I really have a terrible time with it, Lord, I do.

But I see so much of it—it seems to be happening all the time. Tell me, Lord, how to deal with it—what should I do?

I see people dying.

And then I see people who wish that they could die.

And I'm caught in between them.

What is it, Lord? Why do things have to be that way?

I'm confused, Lord. Please help me to understand. Please, help me. O.K.?

I will speak in the anguish of my spirit; I will complain in the bitterness of my soul. **Job 7:11**

Dear Lord, sometimes life
doesn't go too well, and
it's times like that that
I cry out to you, like
David who prayed:

"Out of the depths I cry to you, O Lord,
Lord, hear my prayer."

And I cry out to you Lord,
for suffering, starving
people; people who are
being destroyed by the
selfishness and greed
of other people.

Lord, Lord hear my prayer and help them.

Lord, you are my only hope.
And Lord, you are their only hope.

Please, Lord, help them.
Save them from the hands of the unjust.

Inspired by Ps. 130

Lord God, I feel so angry I think I am liable
to hit the next person I meet
right in the mouth!

This anger is such a volatile thing,
such an unexpected thing, and I must admit,
a thing that I do not like.

Help me, please, to deal with it,
help me to express it in a good way,
a right way.

Help me, Lord, help me to rise above
such feeling.

Help me to understand what I'm about
to do next.

Help me to understand who I am when
I'm like this.

"Out of my distress I called to the Lord, and He
answered me."   Jonah 2:3

Lord, I feel the weight of suffering.
*   I see it all around me.*

There are so many struggling, hurting people.

There is a young woman hurt very much by a love relationship that's going sour.

There is a mother of nine children who experiences the constant pain of multiple sclerosis.

There are two people whose lives have been shattered because walls grew up between them and now divorce seems the only way out.

There are many, many people suffering terribly for mistakes they've made.

I pray to you, Lord, help them. Support them.

Let them experience your love.

"O, that I might have my request and that God would grant what I long for."   **Job 6:8**

*Lord God, over the last few days this school
has not been a pleasant place to be.*

*Vandalism has always been terribly
upsetting to me for some reason.
I can remember quite well that it
upset me even when I was a student
in high school.
But what really upset me—
yesterday—was student reaction to it.*

*So many kids seemed to think that
it was funny.*

God, was that ever depressing!!

*Help me, Lord, to live with this.
Help all of us, Lord, to look at
ourselves as others see us.*

*Give to us the grace of knowing
ourselves, both the good and the
not-so-good.*

*And then inspire us to get off our
lazy back-ends and do something
about it.*

Please, Lord??

**There are just men treated as though they had done
evil and wicked men treated as though they had done
justly.   Eccl. 8:14**

thanking

Lord God, I thank you for gentle people—people
who can hear what I say
> *and then say*
>> *that it's all right that I said*
>> *what I said.*

Lord, I don't care for people who laugh at me,
and say stupid, empty things
> *about how*
>> *what I said*
>>> *doesn't*
>> *really count for anything.*

But I do want to say "thank you" to you
for making so many people around me
who are willing to affirm who I am.
I'm grateful to you, too, for helping me
tolerate the other kind of people who,
for fear of themselves, want to cross out
the possibility of my existence.
Thank you, Lord, for life—
help me tolerate destruction.

...If I have no love I am a noisy gong, a clanging cymbal. **I Cor. 13:1**

Thank you, Lord, for love.

I'm thinking of people
      who can look outside
      of themselves
      and recognize
      another human being—
         a person—
      a person who also
      hungers and thirsts,
         a person—
      a person who
      needs and feels,
             wonders
               &
            gets surprised.

For these people, Lord, I thank you.

Help me, Lord, to love as they do.

Finally, Lord, please, be with my Dad
right now as he faces some
pretty serious surgery.
I love him, Lord, please help him.

Beloved, let us love one another because love is of God.   **I Jn. 4:7**

Lord, I hear your voice in the sounds of spring.

> I hear you when I hear rain falling
> softly on the roof.

> I hear you while I listen to the sound
> of the thunder as it booms out the crash
> and smash of nature rejuvenating itself.

Lord, I see you when I see green grass
and budding trees.

> I see you when I see farmers out plowing
> the fields and disking corn stalks.

Lord, I can feel you as I drive down a highway
and the wind is blowing across my face.

> I can feel you when I leave my jacket
> at home and still am warm.

> I can feel you when the sun is
> hot on my face.

Lord, I thank you for showing yourself to me,
demonstrating your power and letting me
experience your kindness and gentleness.

Lord, I am grateful. I am!

**It was I who made the earth and created mankind
upon it.**   **Is. 45:12**

Lord, I thank you for people.

Beautiful people.

People who know how to love.

I thank you, so graciously,
for people who listen,
           think,
           care,
           trust,
           take a chance.

I thank you for people
who want to know more,
           hear more,
           experience more,
           understand more.

Lord, I thank you for
letting me be next to
such people.

I thank you for people
who love people.

Oh, one more note Lord.

Thank you for the mystery of life.

"I will thank you always for what you have done."
                                          Ps. 52:11

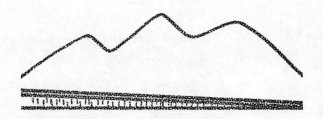

Lord, I praise you.

> *I thank you because you have given us
> so many good things.*

*You have given us the slowly rolling, gradual,
up and down hills of the Linn County landscape.
It is reassuring and comforting in its constancy.*

*And Lord, you have given us the sharp, crisp
bluffs of the Mississippi valley. They are solid
and powerful. They remind me that you are able to
convince me that things are all right
even when I'm upset.*

*O Lord, you have given us this community of
LaSalle. It is characterized by giggles and screams,
and challenges to do even better.*

> *Thank you, Lord, for this.*

*It makes me remember that I can be even more
than I ever was before.*

**. . . A good and spacious land, a land flowing with milk
and honey.**   **Ex. 3:8**

Lord God, I want to thank you
for good steady
reliable people—
people you can
count on.

I'm not thinking of
the flashy people who
have hot moments now
and then.

I'm not thinking of
"cool" people who
never get excited
about anything or
anybody but themselves.

I'm thinking about people
you can go to after the hot-shots,
the hot-dogs
and the hot-potatoes
have all turned cold and clammy.

I'm thinking about friends who
are still friends after you've
done something stupid and
socially unacceptable.

I'm thinking about people who have
patience and love—people who care
about somebody besides themselves.

Thank you, Lord, for the good,
steady, reliable people.

Instead, seek after integrity, piety, faith, love, steadfast-ness, and a gentle spirit.   **I Tim. 6:11**

Thank you, Lord, for Fridays.
I need the time and the space to unwind, to think,
to pray, to catch up.

And, thank you, for the nice warm days
that come after cool crisp evenings.
I love them both.

Thank you for football games and bonfires,
for long, late, late into-the-evening chats,
for old friends that come back again.

Thank you for canoe trips and cookouts.

Thank you for the crunch of dead leaves underfoot.

Thank you for hayrides, oh yes, especially for
hayrides.

Thank you for gladdening the hearts of your people.

"We keep on thanking God ..."   **II Thess. 1:2**

Lord God, I thank you for quiet times.

> I appreciate the beauty of silence,
> because it is in this silence that
> I hear you speak to me.

I hear you tell about the mystery of life.

I hear answers to those great big questions.

I hear you tell me that I am alive and well,
that I am all right.

It is so good to hear this from you, Lord,
so very good.

Thank you, Lord.

Thank you for silence, thank you for speaking to me.

"My love shall never leave you, nor my covenant of peace be shaken, says the Lord." Ps. 54:10

Lord God, I pray to you for growth. Help me to understand myself and what I do.
Give direction to my life.

And Lord God, I thank you for being so generous to me. You have given me so much. You have helped me to see,

> *to believe,*
>
> *to know,*
>
> *to understand,*
>
> *to love.*

It is a rich and beautiful gift that you have given me when you called me to be a priest.

I thank you, Lord. I thank you always even when I don't feel like it.

May grace, mercy, and peace be yours from God the Father and Christ Jesus our Lord.   **I Tim. 1:2**

Lord, we're happy.
It's a good feeling we have when we tell ourselves:
    "We're in the State Tournament!"

Help us, Lord, to reflect a bit on this.
What does it all mean?

> *It means for one thing that we have achieved*
> *something pretty good.*

> *It means that we can do.*

> *It means that some teamwork has happened*
> *and some real cooperation has taken place.*

We pray fervently, Lord, that we may learn
a lot from this.

May we know, please, that we are good—not only
at turning out a good basketball team,
but that we are also good at being human beings.
Maybe we're also good at being Christian people.

> *We're grateful, Lord,*
> *for this lesson.*

> *We're grateful, Lord,*
> *for the chance*
> *to show everyone*
> *that we are good.*

> *Give us the courage, Lord,*
> *to prove all of this again.*

Come, children, hear me, I will teach you the fear of the Lord. **Ps. 34:12**

O Lord, I'm grateful to you
because you have been so good to me.

You heard me when I cried out to you
in the anguish of my despair
and loneliness.

I begged you for an end to my suffering
and you granted it to me.

And now, Lord, I praise you and thank you.

I think thoughts like: "How good the Lord is to me."

"He hears me and he answers me."

Lord, I praise you and thank you.
Only one thing I ask:

When I suffer again, help me to remember
and cherish this time of happiness.

God is my strength; He makes my feet swift as those
of hinds, He enables me to go upon the heights.
Hb. 3:19

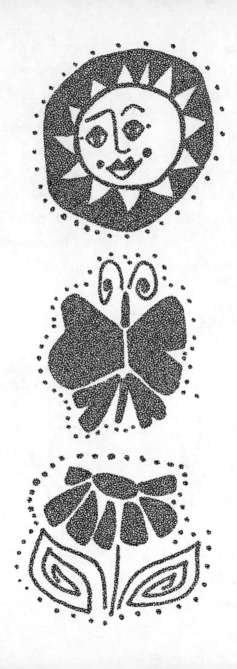

*Let's take a little time out to THANK God
for all the good things we have.*

*We thank you, Lord God our Father, for the
beauty of our world.
We praise you when we see your sunlight
mirrored off the white frost clinging
to naked tree branches.
We thank you, Lord God our Father, for
the goodness of our school.
We praise you when we see girls and boys play
good basketball.
We praise you when we see our young
freshmen take upon themselves a successful
clothing drive for the poor.
We praise you when we see and hear students
sing beautiful songs as they prepare for
a thing called a Madrigal.
We praise you, Father, when it occurs to us
that there are many people, call them all
teachers, who work hard to make our school
a real school of joy and learning.
We praise you, Father, when we see students
thrilled with the experience of knowing more.
We praise you, when we are aware of students
and teachers working hard to cooperate
with each other.
We praise you, Father, and thank you from
the depths of our lives, when we see, even
in the middle of troubles and hassles,
some really good things going on.*

Can it indeed be that God dwells among men on earth?
I Kgs. 8:27

Lord God, Father of us all, we thank you.
We thank you

> —*for a whole week of school*

> —*for friends who love us and aren't afraid to tell us so*

> —*for students who are good enough to get themselves turned on to learning*

> —*for teachers who delight in watching kids turn on to learning*

> —*for a highly successful Muscular Dystrophy Marathon*

> —*for a beautiful, relaxing 3-day weekend*

> —*for a new school year full of hope and promise.*

I intend to recall these things to you constantly....
II Pt. 1:13

Lord, we praise you, we thank you.

We praise you for big wide beautiful blue skies.

We thank you for sight so we can see the sky.

We praise you for the feeling of crisp, cool evenings.

*We thank you for the freedom we have
to walk around our neighborhoods
without the fear of being mugged,
harrassed or killed.*

*We have been blessed Lord,
we praise you and thank you.*

*But Lord, we ask you to give all
of us your gentleness and your
strength so that we can keep it
this way; so that we don't become
muggers, thieves, or killers.*

*And Lord, we ask you to give this kind of freedom
and peace to others who do not have it.*

**Lo, I am about to create new heavens and a new
earth.**   **Is. 65:17**

Thank you, Lord, for the week off. I was getting pretty cranky before this nice break.

Thank you, Lord, for leading me to quiet, peaceful, happy places like Wild Cat Mountain Park. It was great. And the activity there was just what I needed—just what I liked.

Thank you, Lord, for a day to be by myself. It helped me to understand who I am, especially who I am as I stand before you. I think I see you not so much as someone who judges me, but rather as someone who loves me.

Thank you, Lord, for the three days in Tama, and the time to think about the mystery of your death and resurrection. I really liked it.

Thank you, Lord.

How great are your works, O Lord! How very deep are your thoughts.   **Ps. 92:6**

Lord God, I am grateful to you.

> *I am grateful for new stuff.*

I don't mean a new car.

I don't mean any new furniture.

I don't mean new clothes.

I don't mean new things at all.

Lord, I'm grateful to you for new friends,

> *new experiences,*
>
> *new loves,*
>
> *new excitement.*

Thank you, Lord, for a new me.

I had been waiting and wishing something new would happen to me, and Lord, it did! Thank you!

Do not lay up for yourselves an earthly treasure. . . . Make it your practice instead to store up heavenly treasure.
Mt. 6:19

THE LORD IS GRACIOUS AND MERCIFUL,
SLOW TO ANGER AND OF
GREAT KINDNESS.
THE LORD IS GOOD TO ALL
AND COMPASSIONATE TOWARD
ALL HIS WORKS.

PS 144:8

Let us pray.

Lord, I find great comfort in these words. I do because I know I need your mercy. I am sorry for all the times I have disobeyed you and offended you. Please, do be merciful to me.

Lord, I'm very grateful to you because you have shown your mercy to me.

And, finally, Lord, help me and everyone else in everything we do.

Jesus

is the
greatest !

The gospel of John ends with these words:

NOW, THERE ARE MANY OTHER THINGS
THAT JESUS DID. IF THEY WERE ALL
WRITTEN DOWN ONE BY ONE I SUPPOSE
THAT THE WHOLE WORLD COULD NOT HOLD
THE BOOKS THAT WOULD HAVE
TO BE WRITTEN.

> Lord God, Our Father, we thank you
> for your son, Jesus Christ.
> He is the greatest.
> And the whole thought of God
> becoming a man is so mind-blowing
> that I know all of the arrogance
> and vanity of all humans everywhere
> put together could not have dreamed
> up so fantastic an idea.
> It's really something!
>
> Lord, we can't properly say thanks.
> The best thing that we can do,
> however, in response, is to accept
> and appreciate this beautiful
> act of love.
>
> Thank you, Lord.

FREEDOM

FREEDOM

FREEDOM

freedom

freedom

FREEDOM

FREEDOM

freedom

freedom

Let's consider what God does for us,
and what we do for God.

God has been very good to us. He gives us
many good things. One great gift that God
gives us is freedom. Now it's usually our own
free choices that get us into trouble,
but then it's also through our own free choices
that we are able to do some really great
and good things ourselves.

This freedom we have means that we have
control over who we are, and it also means
that we have a responsibility about who we are.

Somebody said, "What we are born with is
God's gift to us, what we make of ourselves is
our gift to God."

Now—considering this—let us pray:

Thank you Lord for the free will that you
have given to each of us. This freedom to decide
is a great big beautiful thing.
But it can also be awesome and fearful.
We don't always use this freedom rightly.
We beg you, Lord, to help us—guide us along
right paths, inspire us to become good and
upright before you. We're afraid, Lord, of our
mistakes ... but we can also be
very happy with our growth.
Make us happy, Lord.
Help each of us to overcome the fear.

Thank you, Lord.

Know that the Lord is God; He made us, His we are.
Ps. 100:3

Thank you, Lord, for good happy times.

> *I'm thinking about times when people
> let their defenses down and really
> become themselves.*

Sometimes folks are too serious.

> *Then they can talk only about dark
> heavy stuff.
> Then they criticize and complain.
> This hurts.*

And other times they are so silly:

> *drunk-like, stupid and empty.
> At times like this they are
> usually phoney.
> They aren't having a good time,
> they are only trying to.
> They want it so desperately
> that they fake it.*

But thank you, Lord, for the good times.

> *Times when people really truly enjoy life.
> It is so good.*

> *I figure you must be present then and
> laughing along with everybody.*

"Let the heavens be glad and let the earth rejoice."
I Cor. 16:31

*Well, Lord, we're just about at the
   end of the school year*

*And this causes me to reflect
   on the whole year.*

Thank you for being with us when we tried to learn.

*Lord, there is nothing more beautiful
   than watching a student
   struggling to grow—*

it is an act of creation,

*it is profoundly inspiring
to observe.*

*I thank you, Lord, for allowing me to see it
often this year.*

*Five minutes of this can wipe out
five days of ignorance.*

*Lord, I pray fervently for
   all your people here at school.*

Help them to continue to grow.

Thank you, Lord, for a good year.

**You see a man wise in his own eyes? There is more
hope for a fool than for him.**   **Prov. 26:12**

Loving

Lord, there is so much to know.

I am desperate to know more.

I think I got one little insight this weekend.
It has to do with loving.

When you love someone,
you are happy when they're around;
you might even be terribly excited.
It is good.

But then, when you really love someone,
you go way beyond that;
then you become—not a receiver—
but a giver.

Then you are an open wound for them.

You become vulnerable for them.
You give to them the possibility of hurting you.

I got this insight, Lord God, when I tried
to bring together the meaning of marriage
and the meaning of your Son's death.

Thank you, Lord God, for this insight.

It comforts me.
It inspires me.

**"There is no limit to love's forbearance, to its trust, its
hope, its power to endure."**   **I Cor. 13:7**

145

Lord God, I *want to speak to you about*
             ultimate things—things that really count,
             things that last forever,
             not just for a time.

             I think wisdom outlasts gold and silver,
             Let me have wisdom.

             I'm convinced that love really counts
             and that money counts for very little,
             Let me have love.

Lord God, I *praise you and I will go on*
             praising all of my life.

             This counts for much more
             than my praise of success
             that exists only for a time.

Let me *praise you always and forever.*

"What profit does a man show who gains the whole world and destroys himself in the process?"   Mk. 8:37

My prayer today, Lord, is about LOVE.

We're sorry, Lord, for misusing the word;
but really we are most sorry for misusing
the reality of its meaning.

> *When we use this word please let it be*
> *a firm promise;*
>
> *never let it be a purchase or a bribe*
> *or a challenge.*

Perhaps, Lord, we should only use the word
in prayer, in reference to you.
Then, even if we misuse the word at least
we won't misuse the reality because you,
being LOVE, know; and it's certain that
you cannot be bought or tricked or dared.

> *Help us, Lord, we pray, to LOVE, and to*
> *LOVE you, and to LOVE LOVE.*

Let us love in deed and truth, and not merely talk about it.   **I Jn. 3:18**

Thank you, Lord, for loving me.

*I've been especially conscious
of that the last few days.*

*I've been conscious of your love
in so many ways:*

— *in crowds of high school students
having a good time.*

— *in the beautiful weather.*

— *in hearing from some close friends
I have missed lately.*

— *in seeing some young people really
find themselves in your love.*

— *and in finding myself able to commit myself
to you once again.*

*Thank you, Lord Jesus, for loving me.
I really appreciate it.*

**Blessed be the Lord, the God of Israel, through all
eternity! Let all the people say, Amen! Alleluia!**
I Chron. 16:36

Lord God,

help me to be conscious

of whoever is next to me
at this moment.

Tell me, Lord,

to look over at that person
and smile.

Show me, Lord, that that person
is a lot like me.

That person can feel good
or feel bad
just like me.

Show me, Lord, that person.

Teach me to be aware of him or her.

When a person strikes you on the right cheek, turn and offer him the other. Mt. 5:39

Love

Love

Love   Love

Love

Love   Love

Love   Love

Love

Love

Lord, I pray today for your presence in my life.

Give to me the grace of your patience, your love.

If love is gentle and kind,
then I figure I should be
gentle and kind.

But, Lord, it is not always easy
for me to do this. I fail often.
Sometimes I am rude, sometimes
I am unkind.

Inspire me, Lord, today to really be
gentle and kind, patient and loving.

Thank you, Lord.

Love is patient; love is kind ... Love is not rude, love is not self-seeking. I Cor. 13:4-5

Dear Lord, I'm grateful to you for the good friends
that I have—especially the one good
friend who is in my mind now.

This man is with me in my life.
I don't have to stand alone.
I know that and it is the most
beautiful knowledge that I could
ever possess.

A very beautiful side-effect of this knowledge, Lord,
is that it signifies the same kind of knowledge
that I have of you.

The relationship between me and this person
tells me, Lord, of the relationship
between you and me.

Since he cares for me and stands with me,
then I know that you do too.

And, Lord, that is fantastic.

Really fantastic!

**And in his love for David, Jonathan received his oath
to him, because he loved him as his own self.**

I Sam. 20:17

Jesus came to us out of love:
>> *to show us the path to His Father.*

He did it to show us how to love our
>> *fellowman, and the perfect*
>> *example is His Passion, Death,*
>> *and most important,*
>> *His Resurrection.*

Without the Resurrection the rest would
>> *have been in vain.*
>> *Because He rose, He conquered*
>> *death and sin for the world.*

He did it so that we too could have power
>> *over sin and death,*
>> *if we follow His path.*

Because Jesus did go through it, our lives
>> *have purpose and direction,*
>> *if we try to live in His way.*

Lord, help us, help us to live in your way.

We have a great High Priest who has passed through the heavens, Jesus, the Son of God.   Heb. 4:14

Lord, I'm happy.
You have blessed me—you have been so good to me.
And, Lord, you know, I don't always feel this way.
But beautiful people, call them friends,
            have spoken to me and ... well ...

  I'm happy.
  And I'm grateful.

Please, Lord, (and here, I'm asking again)
        but please, Lord, don't let me forget
            moments like this:

            moments when I really feel
            like I'm with you,

            when I'm into life at its best,

            when I'm among people who love me.

Lord, help those who never feel this way.

        Help those who won't let themselves feel
        this way.

Lord, they need your love so much.

Please, Lord, help them.

Seek eagerly after love. Set your hearts on spiritual gifts.   I Cor. 14:1

*Lord God, I love you with my whole
heart and soul—*

*I love you with all that I am.
I love you.*

I want to promise you me.

*I want to give to you my whole person,
all my work,
    my efforts,
    my possessions,
all that I am and
all that I have.*

*You see, Lord, I figure that whatever,
whoever I am is a gift that you have
given to me.*

*And it is also the dearest gift that
I can offer—*

Therefore it's what I offer to you.

*Accept me, possess me, use me for whatever
purpose you want, because I am yours.*

Lord, I love you.

Father, into your hands I commend my spirit. Lk. 23:46

wondering

Lord God, I'm wondering
about all that your son Jesus did—

how He tried so hard to tell us of your
love for us,

and how He spent Himself and finally
gave Himself—really gave Himself totally.

This is good.

One thing that kind of stands out in my mind
as I think about it was His willingness to do
what you wanted Him to do

and His willingness to do
what He knew He must do.

This is beautiful,
especially when I see that Jesus
following His own destiny;

and Jesus doing your will

came, in the end, to be the very same thing.

That is great, Lord God.

I pray that someday I, too, may arrive
at some kind of oneness with you like this.

Lord, let me arrive!

How long, O Lord ... will you hide your face from me? **Ps. 13:2**

Well, Lord, today I'm thinking and wondering
about life. Some riddles, some questions
have come into my mind.

Why am I alive, and not somebody else in my place?

Why is life sometimes so good
and then sometimes not?

Why are some people so horribly cruel,
while others are so gentle and kind?

What the heck is love really all about?

What would I be like if I were somebody else?

This is all kind of crazy, isn't it, Lord?
But then, I suspect you'd agree with me
that there are things a lot worse than being crazy!

I am not God, that I should prevail.   **Prov. 30:1**

Lord, I wonder about the meaning of life.

*For some people, I know, life is
a crazy blast—one high after
another, one party after another.*

*And for some other people,
life is a terrible disappointment—
one bad break after another, one
tragedy after another.*

*And then for yet some others
life is a discovery of new
experiences and new people.*

These folk survive sorrow and pain.

*They relish joy and excitement
without busting their heads
to achieve it.*

*These are the happy—really
happy people.*

Lord, make me one of them.

**Chastised a little, they shall be greatly blessed, because
God tried them and found them worthy of Himself.**
Wis. 3:5

Lord,
sometimes I wonder
what life after death
will be like.

And sometimes I wonder if we Americans
don't work way too hard.

And sometimes I wonder if anybody really
cares about life in outer space.

And then,
at other times
I wonder if anybody else ever wonders about
any of the goofy things I wonder about.

Anyway, Lord,
I usually get a
big kick out of
wondering, and
I'm glad you arranged
it so it's possible
for me to wonder.

Thank you.

It's nice.

"Come and see the works of God. His tremendous deeds among men." **Ps. 66:5**

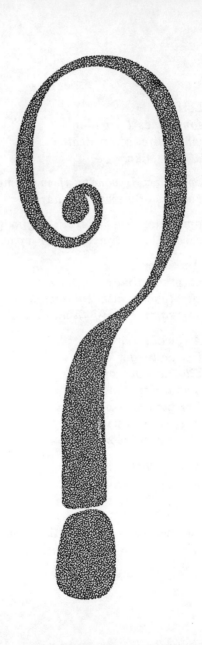

Dear Lord, I'm wondering,
questioning,
moody again.

I'm wondering
about life and
its problems.

I wonder, Lord, is it really
true that making a lot of
mistakes means that a person
is only too human?

I wonder, too, Lord, why does a
great nation, dedicated to
liberty and justice for all,
have to work so terribly hard
to defend itself from its enemies?

And tell me this, Lord:
if people really are made
to love each other, why do they
keep on offending each other,
and defending themselves
from each other?

Why, Lord, if Mass is truly
a celebration, why do so many
people show up for it so reluctantly.

Well, these are just some questions,
Lord. I hope I'm not just
giving you a hard time.
I also want to say that I love you
and I'm very happy that you love me.

**They shall beat their swords into plowshares, and their
spears into pruning hooks.**   **Is. 2:4**

Lord God, I seek understanding.

There is this huge world around me and I want to know what it is, especially I'd like to know the meaning of it all.

Are the stars really as big as the big people tell us?

Is it true that the sun is one huge ball of fire?

Did you really put all the animals and stuff here on earth just for our use, or is it conceited of us to think that?

Lord, this is really something else! If you have all this stuff now—what will you have for us to look at in a few billion eons?

I like to wonder about all this— But, I guess I really don't need any answers right now.

"Come! behold the deeds of the Lord, the astounding things He has wrought on earth." Ps. 46:9

Lord, I feel, deep inside of me, a feeling of wonder, of awe.

It's like the feeling I had when I saw a mountain for the first time.

It's like the feeling I had the first time I said Mass.

This feeling of wonder came to me because I've been thinking about beautiful things like the wind murmuring, the autumn leaves rustling, sea-gulls flapping their wings, and waves of water washing ashore.

I love this feeling, Lord, and I thank you for it.

I am amazed.

You gave to me all of these beautiful things and then, as if that weren't enough, you also made me able to feel this wonder.

"Come and see the works of God...."   Ps. 66:5

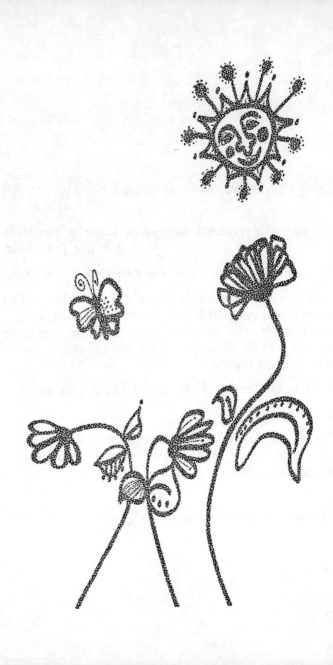

Lord God, I appreciate the life you
          have given me.

               I understand that it is
               a mystery, this life;
               and as such I am intrigued by it.

               I am full of wonder
               at the endless possibilities I have.

               I stand here, breathless
               because of all that has been given me;
               and I figure that that is
               next to nothing
               compared to what is still
               in store for me.

               I am mindful of St. Paul's words:

"EYE HAS NOT SEEN, NOR EAR HEARD,
NOR HAS IT EVEN ENTERED INTO THE
MIND OF MAN WHAT YOU HAVE IN STORE
FOR THOSE WHO LOVE YOU."

                                        I Cor. 2,9

Thank you, Lord, for this dazzlingly
beautiful possibility.

Lord God, I wish to speak
to you today about where
I think you are.

Since you are a father,
I think you are present
wherever people realize
their brotherhood.

If you are a Creator,
I think you're bound
to show up wherever
creation is going on,
whether that be out
in the farthest galaxy,
or in the closest cell
of my body.

Since you are Lord of heaven and earth,
you're probably on the spot to any
human person who admits that he's not
King of Everything.

So, when I pray to you
God, I want to say to
you that I acknowledge
you as being wherever
life is. I acknowledge
that you are my personal
Lord, my dear loving
Father, and my own very
responsible Creator.

And, that's
just all
right with me.

There is cause for rejoicing here.   **I Pt. 1:6**

172

Lord God, help me to understand—give me
an answer to some questions.

Why do we Americans spend more money on
cosmetics than we do on helping the poor?

Why do people who profess to love each other
spend so much time and energy hurting each other?

Why do young people sometimes build barriers
against adults at the same time as they are
rapidly becoming adults themselves?

And why do so many adults pretend so earnestly
that they were never teenagers?

Why do some people insist on going to school
when they absolutely don't want to learn anything?

And Lord, how can I sometimes yearn
so fervently for you, and then at other times
manage to keep you out of my life?

> *It's funny, Lord, it's*
> *really peculiar how we*
> *humans can be so smart*
> *and so dumb at the same*
> *time.*

What did you have in mind when
you made us like this?

Are you maybe trying to tell us something?

Maybe several things, things like faith, hope, love,
> *a sense of humor,*
> *a sense of wonder,*
> *an experience of mystery?*

I will restore you to health, your wounds I will heal,
says the Lord.   **Jer. 30:17**

Well, Lord, I'm thinking about a
funny, out-of-date, weird subject.

The subject is JUSTICE.

And I'm wondering what it is.

Last night, Lord, I watched a movie called
Walking Tall.

During this movie I heard a man say,

"I believe in equality just as much as anybody.
I just don't want it forced on me."

And I thought, Lord: how often have
I thought or ever said something just
as stupid!

JUSTICE is for everyone, and everytime
that someone is not treated with
JUSTICE, then I lose.

Lord, help me, not simply to understand
this, but, oh, good Lord, help me to live it.

If you bring your gift to the altar and there recall that
your brother has anything against you, leave your gift
at the altar, go first to be reconciled with your brother,
and then come and offer your gift.   Mt. 5:23-24

ALBA ▲ BOOKS

INSPIRING
READING

— — — — Cut around dotted line — — — — —

Are there ALBA BOOKS titles you want but cannot find in your local stores? Simply send name of book and retail price plus 60¢ to cover mailing and handling costs to:
   ALBA BOOKS, Canfield, Ohio, 44406.

Please send: ....
(book titles)

....
            (prepayment   required)

.... ALBA BOOKS general Brochure.

NAME _____

ADDRESS _____

CITY _____ **STATE** _____ **ZIP** ____

ALBA BOOKS

SOCIAL PROBLEMS

SEXUAL MORALITY

PRAYER

MINISTRY

- - - Cut around dotted line - - -

first class
permit no. 49
canfield, ohio

Business Reply Mail
No postage stamp necessary
if mailed in the United States
Postage will be paid by

ALBA BOOKS

CANFIELD, OHIO 44406
Phone: (216) 533-5503

JESUS CHRIST, THE GATE OF POWER by
Earnest Larsen, C.SS.R. — meeting with
Jesus is like falling in love with the girl
next door: you have always known her
— and Him — and yet . . . birds begin to
sing in the treetops, white clouds sail
across the sky and tomorrow is going to
be a splendid day!

Fr. Larsen writes beautifully about Jesus
the REALITY — not Jesus the RITE, which
is what most of us experience. We know
ABOUT Jesus but we seldom KNOW
HIM. What do "Savior," "Community,"
"Baptism," "Redemption" and other fa-
miliar words signify? Read the profound
and sensitive replies to these and many
other questions in this fine volume.

$1.75

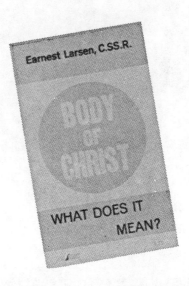

Earnest Larsen, C.SS.R.

BODY
OF
CHRIST

WHAT DOES IT
MEAN?

BODY OF CHRIST by **Earnest Larsen,
C.SS.R.** — Splendid, modern reflections,
enriched by apt illustrations, on the
everyday reality of the Eucharistic Sac-
rament which is inseparably linked to
the flesh and blood Sacrifice of Calvary
and which the author with great sensi-
tivity leads us to find as surely in the
tenement as in the Tabernacle.

$1.75

JESUS I WANT TO TALK WITH YOU by Edward Carter, S.J. — all aspects of every day are of interest to Jesus and He wants us to talk to Him about them. He does not want "formal" prayers but our own words — we do not "read" our remarks to other people, so why to Him? An excellent book for those who want to pray but don't know where to begin or what to say.

$1.95

THE JESUS EXPERIENCE by Edward Carter, S.J. — The "institutional" Church may be in difficulties, but its Founder, Jesus, is riding the crest of a new wave of popularity. In this age, avid for "experiences," Fr. Carter writes movingly of the one experience which produces permanent effects: meeting Jesus.

$1.75

Are there ALBA BOOKS titles you want but cannot find in your local stores? Simply send name of book and retail price plus 60¢ to cover mailing and handling costs to: ALBA BOOKS, Canfield, Ohio, 44406.